No Hope Beyond This Point

(A Collection of Short Stories)

No Hope Beyond This Point (A Collection of Short Stories)

Copyright © 2020 by Nicki Snyder.

ISBN (kdp): 9781653310838
ISBN (print copy): 978-1-955762-00-7
ISBN (ebook copy): 978-1-955762-03-8

Front cover image by Nicki Snyder.

Published by TheShyWriter
www.theshywriter.org

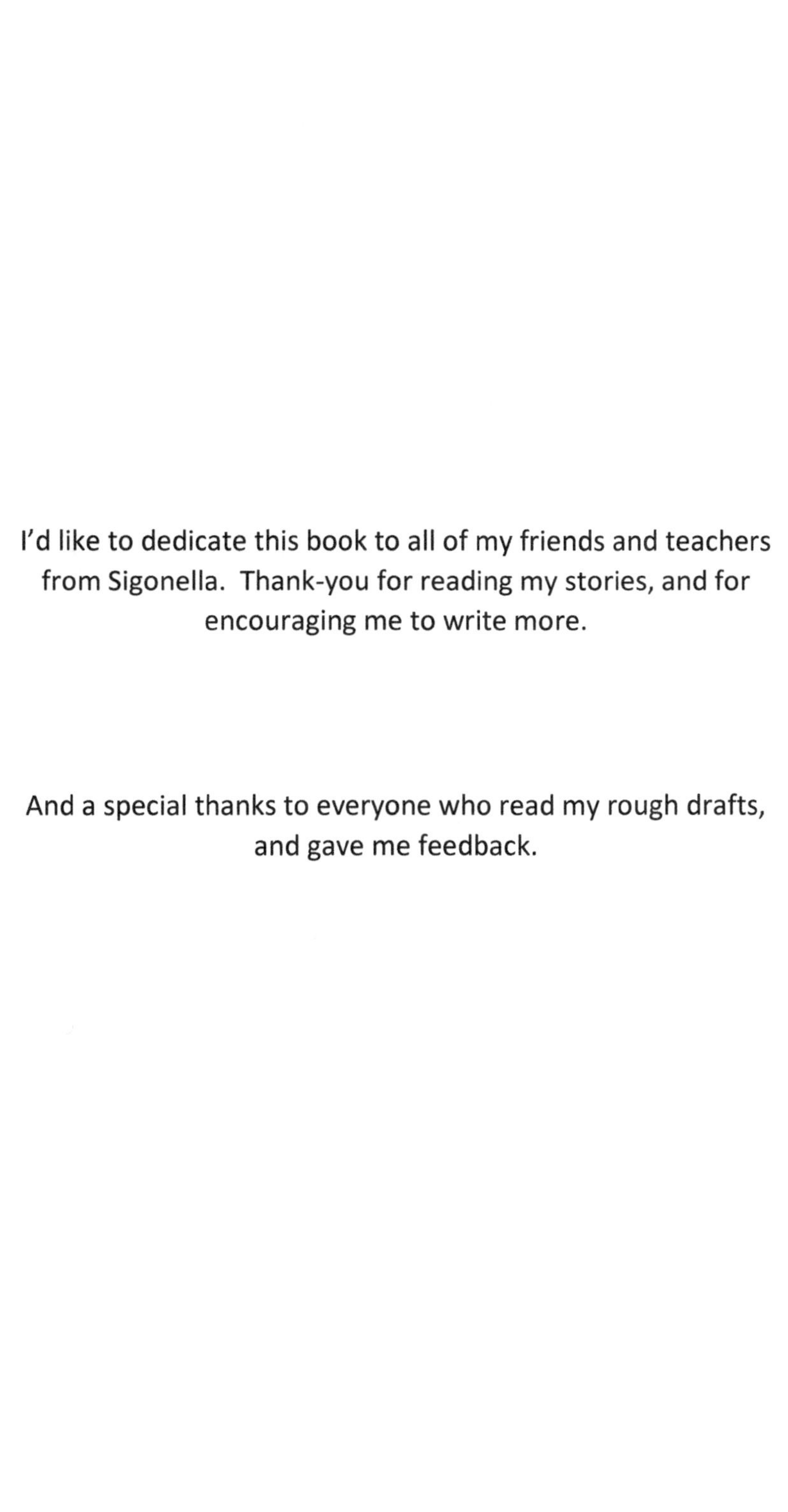

I'd like to dedicate this book to all of my friends and teachers from Sigonella. Thank-you for reading my stories, and for encouraging me to write more.

And a special thanks to everyone who read my rough drafts, and gave me feedback.

Table of Contents

Introduction

No Hope Beyond This Point is the first non-children's book that I've published. However, a few of the tales included were written before any of my other publications.

The short stories inside are an anthology of creepy tales, all born from my overactive imagination, and love of the spooky.

As a kid, I read a lot. When I was 10, I moved back in with my mother. Her boyfriend was an avid reader, too. He owned many Stephen King books, which my mom gave the ok for me to read. I devoured them. As soon as I finished one, I'd start another.

Besides Stephen King, my pre-teen and teen years were mostly influenced by authors John Saul and R.L. Stine.

Reading, though, wasn't the only way I took in the horror genre. Watching scary movies and t.v. shows was something I enjoyed doing with my dad. It's a love that I've shared with my sister, and now with my daughter.

My favorite movies were *Nightmare on Elm Street*, *The Shining*, and *The Creepshow*.   And the main scary t.v. shows I watched were: *Are you Afraid of the Dark?*, *Tales from the Crypt*, *Tales from the Dark Side*, and *The Outer Limits*.

When I was in middle school, I started writing my own stories. I'd pass them to my friends between classes, and they'd give them back to me by the end of the day. Every now and then it would be a teacher who returned the story instead.

I worried the teachers wouldn't like the subjects I wrote about, but they were always encouraging. They thought my writings showed promise.

To this day, I'm still thankful for my friends and teachers that took an interest in what I wrote.

I regret, though, that as an adult, I stopped writing for many years. It took me a while to pick it back up.

When I joined a local writers' group, I felt welcomed and energized. This motivated me to start writing again in earnest.

At first, I didn't have much to bring to the group besides my children's books. I decided to take out some old horror stories I had kept, but rarely looked at. With feedback, I reworked them, trying to stay true to what I had originally written. And in the process, I came up with a few new ideas.

I love the type of horror I grew up with. By today's standards it can be a bit tame, but it holds a special place in my heart, and it inspired all of the stories in this book.

I hope you enjoy them, because what's writing without readers to share your work with?

-Nicki Snyder

Do You See Him?

Excuse me, but I have to know.

Do you see him over there?
Across the street?

He's waving at me. Slowly.
He does that a lot.

I made the mistake of waving back once.
He grinned at me.

It was unnatural how far he could stretch his face.
You could see through his smile to the people behind him.
Almost like he wasn't really there.
But he is.

I shouldn't assume.
I only think it's a man.
He's always so far, and shrouded in shadow.
He might not be human at all.

No. Don't back away.
He won't come closer.
He just likes to follow and be where he shouldn't be.
Like now.

He shouldn't be there.
How can he be there?
There isn't even anything for him to stand on.
Yet, there he is.
Hovering over the water of the fountain.

You don't see him, do you?
Well, maybe you can't.

No, don't leave. Don't back away.
Really, it's okay.

It's okay that you don't see him.
It doesn't matter, honestly.

It doesn't matter because I see him.
And... *he sees you*.

Prisoner

Anthony sat rigidly in a corner of the room. His back pressed firmly against the cold, jagged stone. His legs stretched out before him; clad in torn, threadbare, cloth pants.

Another dreary soul occupied the corner closest to him. A man that had marched through the fields with him. A man whose scraggly, hollow appearance, Anthony felt he shared.

And though he and the man had exchanged no words, they were bonded. Bonded by the fact that they were both prisoners; forced here by their captors. Held over for a trial they had little hope of winning.

So far it seemed as if the only true winner here was Death itself.

There had been others in this cell, but one by one Anthony had watched fate choose them until now there were just two.

He did not delude himself into believing those others had survived. He had heard the cries of pain; the sound of people begging for mercy.

Anthony welcomed the silence that followed, wishing it would stay quiet.

When the screams beyond the door were sometimes too much to bear, he'd press the heels of his hands tight against his ears, trying desperately to block out the sounds and the images they brought.

However, too much silence wasn't a good sign either. At those moments, he found himself straining in the dim and drafty cell, trying to hear the faintest noise beyond the thick, wooden door.

Both he and the other man cringed anytime they heard footsteps slowly advancing their way. Relieved sighs escaped them when the footsteps continued past their prison.

The constant stress wore Anthony down, making it hard for him to judge how long he had actually been here. Sometimes he was certain it had been only a few days, but seconds would pass, and he'd convinced himself he'd always been here.

Light streamed in through holes higher up in the wall and ceiling, but it was hazy, making it a poor indicator as to what hour it was. Anthony found himself dozing in and out, which offered a little reprieve, but made it that much more difficult to keep track of time.

He had assumed fighting in the war would prepare him for the possibility of capture, but nothing could prepare him for the waiting. Waiting to be freed, to be spared, to be tortured... to be put to death.

He had lost control of his fate, and that filled him with a sense of finality he had not experienced before. Oh, how he wished they would get it over with, and yet, at the same time, he hoped they would simply forget about him.

He tried to picture himself somewhere else; to recall better days, but his mind kept traveling to dark places.

He saw his comrades fallen on the battlefield, and wondered if they had been the lucky ones, having escaped this horrid confinement.

Despite the agony in his soul, and the haunting images he saw when he closed his eyes, Anthony found himself falling asleep again. He dozed for a while, only to be awoken by a rasping cry of anguish.

His eyes flew open and he stared into the corner near him; terror making his heart beat fast in his chest.

For a brief moment, he thought the corner was empty, but no, his only companion was still there. Anthony began to relax against the stone wall again when he heard it. The sound of heavy footsteps coming closer, almost as if he had willed them.

They stopped on the other side of the door. Dread filled him as the door was pulled opened. A large silhouette of a man stood there. Anthony felt his time had come.

It had not.

The large man barely stepped inside the musty cell before ordering the man in the corner to come forward.

Anthony watched as his only companion inched his way across the small room with terror-filled eyes; creeping low. As soon as he was within a few feet of the silhouette, the guard reached out an arm, grabbed the man, and yanked him to his feet.

Anthony heard a whimper before his cellmate was shoved out of their only safe haven.

The guard slammed the door behind him with such force that it rebounded from the frame; just enough to keep it from latching.

Here was a glimmer of hope, beckoning Anthony. As soon as the footfalls started to fade, he leapt at his one chance for freedom. He stumbled into the door, involuntarily pushing it further open as weakness overtook him. He glanced down a long, narrow hall and saw a few more guards.

Fear made his strength return as he shoved off of the door and ran away from the jailers. Anthony didn't hear anyone coming after him, but he didn't risk looking back.

What he did make time for was to check doors as he went. All of them opened, but only revealed more cells. Dumbfounded, he tried a different passage only to see it blocked by another hulking figure. Anthony slowly retreated but was not followed; merely watched.

He retraced his steps, desperately trying to find an exit. He ran into more guards, or perhaps they were ones he had already encountered.

He was outnumbered, but not ready to give up. After several tense moments, the men stepped aside. Anthony sprinted past them and found a way out. A door was open before him. He could see dirt and smell fresh air, but bars prevented him from continuing.

Anthony slumped against the metal rods. There truly was no escape, a fact he was slowly accepting. A large hand landed on his shoulder. He turned around out of instinct. His jailer was here, and now, finally, it was Anthony's turn.

The Long Drive

Sharlene glances at her watch as she runs down the flight of stairs. She can't make out the time in the dim light cast by the single lamp near the entrance.

At the bottom of the stairs she grabs her keys, wallet, and pack of cigarettes by the door.

She leaves her house and locks the door behind her, briskly walking down the short sidewalk to her car parked in the driveway. She gets in and starts it up.

The clock on the dash reads 9:08 pm. She has plenty of time.

It's chilly outside so she sits in the driveway letting the heater warm the car up. She stifles a yawn and decides to have a cigarette while she waits. She pulls one out, lights it, and draws in a drag as she tosses the cigarette pack into the passenger's seat with her wallet.

She moves her cigarette to her left hand and searches for a good station on the radio. After finding a song she likes, she takes another drag of her cigarette, and leans her head back. Sharlene closes her eyes and listens to the music.

She chastises herself for not taking a nap after her classes were done. She knew her friend was throwing a party tonight.

Stifling a second yawn, Sharlene takes another drag, letting the smoke drift towards the ceiling; her eyes still closed. She rests another minute or two before sitting up with a sigh. Sharlene decides she's let the car idle long enough.

She snuffs out her cigarette in the ashtray, and flicks on her headlights. Sharlene puts her car in reverse and backs slowly down her sloped driveway. She's careful to make sure no one is coming since people speed down this road all the time. And it doesn't help that they haven't installed any streetlights here. *Why would they?* she thinks. *It's not like many people live out here anyways.*

Sharlene puts the car into drive, and heads towards the party on the other side of town.

She sets her cruise control to 55. She's been pulled over one too many times on this stretch of highway. The cops like to hide in the dense vegetation on the side of the road, knowing this is a notorious spot for speeders.

The song she was listening to ends, and the next one causes her to scrunch up her nose. She hates this song. Sharlene reaches forward and pushes the pre-set buttons of the radio. Her focus turns more to her search, and less on the road.

On the fourth try she finds another good tune and straightens up in her seat, only to grab the wheel and hit the brakes. The car rapidly slows down, but doesn't stop. Her headlights catch the tail end of some large shadow as it slinks back into the brush.

Sharlene's heart hammers in her chest as she cruises past the area where she saw the animal disappear. There's no trace of it.

Coming back to her senses, Sharlene's eyes dart to her rearview mirror. *No one there.* She's relieved. *Better get back up to speed before someone rear ends me.*

Taking her foot off the brake, she presses down on the gas until she's up to 55 again. Her eyes briefly flick back and forth to double check that nothing else is trying to jump out of the fields on each side.

During the daytime, it's beautiful out here. Sharlene loves seeing the stalks of corn sway in the breeze; the farmers' fields broken up by wildflowers and trees.

At dusk and dawn, though, it's important to watch for all the critters running out into the road.

What the heck kinda animal was that? Sharlene wonders. *Seemed large. And I'm pretty sure we don't have any bear out here. At least I don't believe we do.*

Sharlene shakes the thought away as another song comes on that she doesn't like. She keeps both eyes focused on the road as she chooses a different station.

I should've passed that old farmhouse by now, Sharlene thinks a few minutes later. She lets out a yawn, then crinkles her brow in concentration. *Yeah, I should be at least a mile past it.* But she can't remember seeing the building. She glances further down the highway to better gauge how far she is when she sees a shadow take shape at the side of the road.

This time Sharlene's prepared. She eases up on the gas and checks that no one is right behind her.

There are no lights in either direction. Just her and whatever creature that is. *Seems too large to be a dog. Some drunk maybe?*

She slows down a little more, her speedometer reading 42. She moves slightly into the other lane in case whatever it is decides to jump out at the last second.

It doesn't.

Instead, it moves back into the undergrowth, just enough to keep her from clearly seeing its shape. Its head, though, follows her car's movement as she passes by.

Sharlene involuntarily shivers. *What was that?* She glances back in her rearview, but all she can see is the red glow of her taillights.

She turns her attention back in front of her and nearly slams on the brakes. It's there; just ahead of her again, off to the side of the road. Her heart pounds in her chest as she squeezes the wheel with both hands.

Her eyes widen as she coasts past the hulking, shadowy creature. It stares at her with eyes that appear black in the glare of the headlights. Sharlene manages to notice it has matted fur, but what color, she couldn't say.

A horn startles her out of her stupor and she glances wildly around for the source.

A large truck is bearing down on her car from behind. She picks up her speed only for the truck driver to blast the air horn again. The semi's lights flood the interior of her car as it gets closer to her bumper. One more honk and it moves into the other lane to pass her.

Sharlene keeps her eyes straight ahead, not wanting a confrontation with the driver as the truck flies past her and into the darkness ahead. Its receding taillights are like fading embers in the night.

Hands tight on the wheel, Sharlene dares to glance at the clock. 9:43 pm. *How am I still on this highway? Did I pass my turnoff?* She looks around for a familiar landmark, but nothing stands out. *I didn't sit in the driveway that long. Maybe for a song or two, but still...*

She keeps her speed at 55, hoping to get out of this wooded area soon, but not desperate enough to risk getting a ticket.

Everything her headlights hit, casts long shadows out into the gloom. She sees movement from every shrub and sapling that whizzes past her windows. Her heart begins to race, and her knuckles turn white as she clenches the steering wheel.

A blur darts out from her left and she turns the wheel away from it. The shape stops short and Sharlene sees that it's only a bunny.

Calm down, she tries to tell herself, but it's hard. *Perhaps it wouldn't be so bad if a cop pulled me over*, she considers. *At least I wouldn't be alone.*

Another blur darts out, and Sharlene begins to veer around it, but it's large. Much larger than she expects, and it quickly moves into her path.

She jerks the wheel, and hits the gravel, pulling her tires off the road. She corrects the car; rocks shooting up from behind.

Sharlene looks out of the driver's side window to see what she nearly hit this time. The creature's face is pressed to the glass. She lets out a shriek and her hands automatically move to cover her eyes; the wheel turning with no one to guide it.

The car lurches back onto the gravel and down into a ditch. Sharlene pitches forward, hard against the steering wheel. Her ribs are bruised. Her body then jerks back as the car comes to an abrupt stop. Her head hits the headrest and her eyes pop open involuntarily.

She looks around, expecting to see the large beast bearing down on her. And for a moment her sleep-addled brain conjures its form.

She shrinks back in fear, then yells as pain seers her leg. The sudden shock causes her to take in her surroundings. She momentarily ignores the agony she feels in her leg as she realizes she's still in her driveway.

The clock above the radio reads 9:21.

What? she thinks before pain brings her back to the present.

"Ow!" Sharlene shouts, finally looking down to see what's biting her. Her hand is resting on her left leg, while the cigarette burns a growing hole into her pants.

She quickly beats the embers off her clothes causing the still smoldering cigarette butt to fall to the floorboard.

Immediately, she bends down to retrieve it, letting up on the brake in the process. In her panic, Sharlene fails to notice that she's moving.

It takes a few moments for her fingers to locate the butt and pull it back up to safety. The car continues to gently roll down the hill.

Sharlene slumps back in her seat, the cigarette butt in her hand. Relief floods through her, but confusion mars her features as the garage door recedes from her.

The car softly thumps into the road, and the sound of an air horn causes Sharlene's head to whip around. Headlights fill her vision as a semi barrels towards her car with no time for either to move.

It hits her broadside, shoving the remains of her car into the brush. The semi jack-knifes across the road.

The smell of burning tires fills the air as blood pools in Sharlene's lungs. The steering wheel is pressed tight against her ribs. Her head aches, and her limbs feel numb. She fights to stay conscious.

Sharlene looks around in a daze, her eyes landing on a dark, matted animal, glaring at her through the windshield.

She tries to move, but is held tight to her seat. She draws in a breath to shout for help but chokes and coughs; blood staining her lips. She watches with wide eyes as it stalks closer to the wreckage.

There's nowhere to go, she realizes.

The large, shadowy monster crunches over the debris with hunger in its coal-black eyes. It moves around her car, and just as it did in her dream, the creature presses its face to her window.

Sharlene tries one more time to scream, but nothing comes out.

She begins to succumb to the darkness encroaching on her vision. Sharlene can still make out the shape of the creature to her side, though. She hears its nails scratch across the car. It seems to be searching for a way in.

She closes her eyes, not wanting to see what will happen if it succeeds in opening the door. *Too late*, she thinks, as the rush of cool air blows across her face.

She hears the squeak of hinges moving, and a low growl near her ear. Sharlene's last sensation is the feeling of wet drool trailing down her arm.

And with that, she welcomes unconsciousness.

Who's There?

A cold wind blows

Howling through the trees

He nestles down under the covers

Hiding from the bitter chill

Branches clatter against the house

Making their presence known

Or are those noises coming from somewhere closer?

He burrows further down

Eyes shut tight. Hands clenching blankets

Who's there? "Dad? Mom?"

Scuttling heard 'cross the floor. His blanket is tugged

"Don't look. Don't peek," he tells himself

Tugging again. A soft weight settles on his legs

"Don't move. Don't breathe. I'll be safe."

Claws felt as it crawls its way up

Nerves get the best of him

Blankets are flung back. The monster revealed

Foul breathe, sharp teeth... hungry eyes

The wind howls. Banshees shriek

An empty bed is found in the morning

The Stall

Rhonda enters the bathroom at work. All the stall doors are closed, but it's silent, suggesting she's alone.

Rather than tugging on the doors to see if a stall is occupied, she bends over and glances down the row, looking for shoes or shadows, and sees that they're all empty.

Straightening up, she heads into the first stall, as she often does out of convenience and habit. The hinges give a slight screech as she pushes the door open, and another when she shoves it closed.

While she sits on the toilet, Rhonda's eyes flit around the compact area, taking in her surroundings. The latch is askew, but still works, so she dismisses it, and there are small chips in the paint on the back of the door.

She lets her eyes travel upward. There are no lights above her, just a dusty vent. The lights are above the sinks and the stall next to hers.

Rhonda scans back down to the wall at her side. The only writing on there is a small sign saying **"Do Not flush trash down the toilet. Place it here."** An arrow points to a small trash can on the floor.

That's when Rhonda sees the side of a shoe in the next stall. She tenses up for a moment trying to recall if she heard someone come in, but can't.

The shoe is worn, the color mostly faded, and a barely legible word is stitched on the side.

It's definitely seen better days, Rhonda thinks. *And what brand is that? I've never seen it before. Sample? Staple?*

The shadow by the shoe never moves. Rhonda pushes aside the eerie feeling it gives her. She needs to get going. Grabbing some toilet paper, she finishes up, flushes, and heads to the sinks to wash her hands.

She turns to the paper towel dispenser, and dries her hands off. Rhonda glances back towards the stalls, but can't see anything from this angle. She frowns.

I don't hear anything now either, but maybe she's just quiet, she considers.

Throwing the paper towel away, Rhonda leaves the restroom, letting the incident fade from memory as she gets on with her day.

****

A few days pass before Rhonda finds herself alone in a public restroom again. She's out picking up a few items when the urge to go hits her.

Once in the bathroom, she heads straight for the first stall, but an "Out Of Order" sign is taped to it.

She backs up and heads for her second choice, the stall at the end. As she passes by the two middle stalls, she notices the doors are ajar.

Rhonda slips into the last one, latches the door, and sits to pee. There are scuff marks on the tiles, and an extra roll of toilet paper on top of the dispenser. In one of the corners she spies a plunger, and hopes that it's not an omen saying this toilet is broken.

That'd be my luck, Rhonda chuckles to herself.

As soon as she's done, she reaches towards the toilet paper, which, in this larger stall, is inconveniently located on the far wall. She freezes with her arm outstretched, her fingers inches away from their destination. She finds it hard to draw in a breath.

This time Rhonda knows no one came in after her. She would've heard something in the silence, but she didn't. And there is no denying the shoe in the next stall, worn and faded, with a word stitched on the side. An "S" and "p" barely visible.

The shadow next door shifts slightly, and Rhonda quickly snatches some toilet paper. From this distance and angle, she can almost see both shoes, and part of the frayed pant cuffs just above them.

She wipes, flushes, and adjusts her clothes, all while staring at the shoes. She refuses to let them leave her sight, until she feels ready to exit.

Rhonda keeps her back to the wall, hoping to catch a glimpse of the shoes as she starts to make her way past the stall next to hers, but stops.

She's momentarily disoriented by the half-open stall door. It's unoccupied. She's sure of it. She pushes the door open just to double check. There are no shoes, no person, no anything out of the ordinary.

Rhonda looks back into the stall she just vacated. It's still empty. She goes down the line, pushing the doors open. Empty, empty, and "Out Of Order". She has to know if this one is empty too, so she bends over to look inside. The floor is bare, but dirty.

Rhonda stands up. She glances towards the sinks and sees that no one's there either. Feeling confused, she stays rooted in her spot. The bathroom door opens as a woman pushes inside. She nearly smacks into Rhonda.

"Oh, excuse me," the startled woman says, giving Rhonda a sideways glance as she moves around her.

"It's alright," Rhonda mutters, moving to the sinks to wash her hands.

She hears the woman go down the aisle and choose a stall. Rhonda dries her hands, but curiosity makes her look to see which stall the woman chose. The third one down. The one that had the shoes.

Carefully, Rhonda leans down to peak at the woman's footwear. She breathes a sigh of relief when black flats come into view.

Those aren't the same ones, she tells herself, standing back up. She drops her paper towel into the trash and leaves, feeling ridiculous.

****

For the next week, Rhonda can't help but feel jittery every time she enters a public bathroom. At work, she's been using the personal one up front, rather than risk being alone in the ones by the breakroom.

After a week goes by with no strange occurrences, she starts to think it was all in her head.

She begins to force herself to use the bathrooms she normally would, whether at work or out shopping.

Nothing strange happens, and life moves on.

****

It's not fair most of the building took the day off, Rhonda grumbles, pushing into the bathroom. *How does everyone seem to have so much vacation time?*

She sits down in the first stall, the door latch still askew, and lets out a sigh. *Wait, was I just complaining out loud?* she worries.

Feeling self-conscious, Rhonda holds her breath for a moment, wondering if someone else is in here. She listens, then glances down. All clear.

She lets her breath out, and chuckles a little at her own behavior. Relaxing, she goes back to the task at hand.

With nothing much to do, she takes in the sounds around her. Rhonda hears the 'drip, drip, drip' of water in the sink, and the soft hum of the vent kicking on. Otherwise, it's silent in the bathroom.

She finishes her business, straightens her clothes, and flushes. Her hand reaches for the latch when she hears the squeak of rubber soles on tile coming from beside her.

Rhonda pauses for a moment, standing there uncertainly, her heartbeat picking up speed. She never heard the door open. It might be a soft swoosh, but it's unmistakable. And with how quiet it is, she would've heard something.

She slowly stoops and glances down, looking for a telltale sign that she's not alone, but doesn't see anything.

Straightening up, she hears the noise again. It's from the stall next to hers. Her eyes go back to the floor. She doesn't see any shoes or a shadow, but she does hear the gentle sound of clothes moving.

There's no one there. You checked. Just leave. You're done anyways, she tells herself, but doesn't move.

Instead, she holds her breath again, straining her ears, trying to make sure she really heard something. But she doesn't hear anything now. No breathing, no shuffling, no one grabbing for toilet paper. And just when she convinces herself it was nothing, she hears an audible exhale.

And it wasn't her.

Rhonda flinches, and lets out a shaky breath. Now she does see a shadow on the floor. It seems to grow a little larger before it moves. A shoe comes into view. One she'd recognize anywhere. And while she still can't tell what color they used to be, she can read the writing now. "Simple."

She quickly releases the latch and jerks the door open, but stops abruptly. There, in front of her, is the occupant of the other stall.

I never heard her move!

Forgetting she has nowhere to go, Rhonda backs up. Her calves hit the toilet seat and she lets out a stifled yell. Her eyes widen as the thing in front of her scuffles forward. A fleshless hand reaches towards her. Rhonda screams.

All that is left of her is a smear of blood on a stall door, where inside, an occupant in worn shoes awaits another visitor.

Creature

Tracy sat on the edge of her bed, huddled in the darkness of her room.

Why couldn't her stepmother leave her alone?

Every time her father left, her "new mother", as he called her, was there with an evil glow in her eyes, and a horribly wicked smile plastered on her face.

Oh, how Tracy hated the basement! It was so dark down there, and it contained that awful creature!

It belonged to her stepmother, Juli. And though she had never seen it, Tracy knew it was always close by, waiting for her "mother" to give the signal when it would be okay to strike.

The little girl knew that time was coming soon. At night, when her father was out, she could hear the monster's cries of hunger. Lately, the howls had been growing louder, and coming closer to the basement door in the kitchen.

Her stepmother loved sending her down into the basement to fetch various items. The last time Tracy went, she was halfway up the stairs when she heard the door slam shut.

She had just stood there, not sure what she should do next. Eventually, she had slowly crept up the stairs.

Standing on the stoop, she had tried the knob. When it wouldn't turn, panic flooded her. She pounded on the door several times before her stepmother opened it.

Juli had acted surprised, but Tracy knew that she had closed the door on purpose, trapping her down there.

****

There was a loud knock on her door, pulling Tracy out of her memories. The door was flung open, letting the light from the hall flood into her room.

"How many times have I told you not to sit in the dark? It's bad for your eyes! Come here!" Juli yelled, grabbing the little girl by the arm.

She yanked Tracy out of her bedroom, pulling her down the hallway, only stopping when they got into the kitchen. Juli jerked the basement door open and shoved her stepdaughter inside. She shut the door, locked it, and walked away.

Tracy sat on the landing at the top of the stairs, curled up by the door. She started to cry. Tears streamed down her face. She wished she could turn on the light, but the pull chain was at the bottom of the staircase. She didn't think it would work anyways. Tracy was sure her stepmother had removed the lightbulb.

She listened to the sounds beyond the door, and to the ones from down below. She didn't hear her "mother", but she could hear the sound of something large scuffling along the basement floor. The noise came closer, paused, then moved away.

Tracy waited for her eyes to adjust to the dim light. She rubbed her tear-stained face. Her heart hammered in her chest.

Once she realized Juli wasn't coming to let her out like last time, Tracy decided she would have to be brave enough to find a light that worked. And if she was lucky; a way out.

****

Juli crept up and listened closely to the sounds behind the basement door. Even though the door muffled noise, she had heard the faint whimper of crying earlier. Now, she heard nothing. It had been deathly quiet for quite some time.

Carefully, she opened the door. She paused in the entranceway and still heard nothing. She clicked on her flashlight and swept it across the stairwell. She didn't see Tracy anywhere. She had expected the girl to still be cowering on the landing, or better yet… dead.

Frowning, Juli started down the stairs. She didn't think the deed was done.

Near the bottom of the staircase, she saw blood on the steps. A cruel smile curled Juli's lips before she realized that it wasn't enough, which meant the little girl was still alive. Juli moved away from the stairs and began searching the basement.

Keeping very still, Tracy watched from the corner she was in. She stayed hidden while her stepmother slowly moved around the cellar, shining her light behind several boxes, and under the shelves.

Tracy held her cut hand close to her chest.

While creeping down the stairs earlier, she had tripped on the last few steps. As Tracy pushed herself back up, a loose nail had pierced her hand. She hadn't cried out at the pain, but a sudden clawing sound forced her to quickly run and hide.

****

Juli hoped she was wrong about the blood. The creature wasn't often messy, but it did leave evidence of its kills. Perhaps it had eaten Tracy without leaving much behind. Juli had to know for sure, so she moved a little further into the cellar, continuing her search.

Tracy saw her opportunity for escape. As fast as she could, she dashed past Juli.

Her stepmother spun around at the sound of feet pounding on the stairs. She saw the little girl disappear into the kitchen. Before Juli could take more than a step, she heard the basement door slam shut.

Tracy locked the door and ran to her room. She slid under her bed and hid, peering out to see if her stepmother had followed her.

Juli snarled in frustration and marched towards the staircase. The beam of her flashlight illuminated movement to her side. She turned to see a large, shadowy figure looming out of the dark. She ordered the creature back, but there was unease in her voice. It growled at her, sensing Juli's fear.

Dragging its claws along the concrete, the creature shifted closer. Its eyes narrowed and it sniffed the air. Juli took a step back and it lunged at her.

Upstairs, Tracy heard a deep, throaty roar and shut her eyes, scooting further under her bed.

A scream rose through the floorboards.

Tracy pressed her hands tightly to her ears, hoping that the beast would be satisfied now.

Frozen Dreams

The sun is out, a mild breeze blows across the make-shift rink, and there's no sign of snow in the forecast. It's a perfect day for ice-skating.

Katlynn laces up her skates. Her boyfriend is already gliding onto the ice, waiting for her. A few children are staying close to the shore with their parents, while another group is playing an impromptu game of hockey using small branches and a pine cone.

With glee in her heart, and a big grin on her face, Katlynn pushes off the snow-covered grass, and onto the frozen pond.

Her boyfriend, Jason, skates backwards, enticing her to come out further. Katlynn doesn't mind. She's been skating for years; her mother insisted on classes.

She catches up with him, laughing, then playfully shoves him as she races away. For the next hour or so they show off their skating moves to each other.

****

"I don't know about you," Jason says, "but I could use a break."

"Yeah," Katlynn agrees as they head towards the shore.

Subconsciously, she pats her pocket checking that her money is still there. She frowns and takes off one of her white gloves. Reaching into her pocket, her fingers touch nothing but the liner.

Katlynn stops skating and glances around, putting her glove back on.

"What's the matter?" Jason asks, coming alongside her.

"I lost my money. I had two tens, but I must've dropped them somewhere."

"Can't be too far," Jason comments, looking up and down the frozen pond. "I'll help you look."

The pair head off in different directions. Katlynn scans a little further out than they skated, just in case the light breeze blew the tens somewhere else.

After a few minutes, she hears Jason calling for her. She turns around and sees him wave his hand. He's clutching crumpled bills. Katlynn smiles at her boyfriend's good luck, glad he found the money.

She starts skating back, but hits a groove that knocks her off balance. Katlynn falls on her butt. She laughs it off, and starts to get up, brushing off her pants. As she does, she notices something underneath her.

She moves the snow and ice shavings out of the way with her hand. A bloated face looks up, and a scream erupts from Katlynn.

Jason skates up to her, worry stamped on his face.

All Katlynn can do is cry and point to the spot she saw the dead person.

Jason bends over, peering at the ice, then at Katlynn. "What?" he asks.

Wiping tears off of her face, Katlynn looks again, seeing nothing this time.

Jason gives her a concerned look, taking her hand in his. "You okay? Cuz I'm pretty sure you scared everyone here."

She clears her throat, looking back at the ice. There's still nothing there. "Uh, yeah, fine. Sorry." Katlynn smiles at her boyfriend and changes the subject. "Hey, you found my money! Thanks," she says before giving him a quick kiss.

****

Katlynn bolts up in bed. Her hair is disheveled, her breath is coming in quick gasps, and goosebumps cover her arms. She dreamt of the person she saw under the ice. This is the third time this week.

She couldn't make out the features in the dream, just a set of wide, dead eyes that reminded her of a large fish, a white hand pressed up against the ice, and a tangle of dark hair surrounding its face.

****

"Are you up for some skating today?" Jason asks during their phone call.

Katlynn nervously drums her fingers and glances outside. She's said no to Jason the last few times he's asked, but honestly, what was she avoiding?

He didn't see anyone under the ice, and she has to admit, that when she checked again, she hadn't seen anyone either.

"Yeah, I am," she tells her boyfriend.

"Sweet," he replies. "I'll pick you up in a bit then."

Katlynn hangs up, determined to relax and have fun today. No dream is going to chase her away.

****

The day goes well. The couple skate for over an hour with a few of their friends before a shivering, exhausted Katlynn decides to head back, towards the bank.

She plops down close to where several other people are pulling off their skates. Katlynn sits on the edge of the pond with her legs still on the ice. She watches Jason race around with a friend.

After a few moments, she bends her leg, bringing her skate closer, so she can lean forward to untie it. As she does, she looks into the frozen water and sees the dead person staring back at her. Its matted dark hair framing its bloated face. A white hand touching the ice in a plea for help.

With short, panicked breathes, Katlynn shoves herself back off the ice. She scrambles away from the pond then stops herself. A few people are looking at her, including Jason.

Katlynn watches him wave goodbye to his friend before coming over to her.

"See something again?" he asks casually, though the look he gives her reads as unease.

He doubts me, Katlynn thinks. *Fine, then I'll show him.*

"Yes," she admits. "Come here." She grabs his hand and leads him to the pond's edge. "There. Look," she tells him pointing at the ice, keeping her gaze on him.

Jason squats down and looks. He squints at the ice then up at his girlfriend. "Okay, what am I looking at?"

Katlynn peers down. Only dark water and white ice stare back at her. "Never mind," she mutters, before sitting back down and yanking off her skates. She refuses to meet Jason's eyes the whole time.

****

This time when Katlynn wakes up from the dream, she swears she coughs out water, but when she pats her blanket, it's dry. Katlynn can even feel the ice beneath her fingernails. And though the dream is quickly fading, she swears she was digging.

Was I trying to free them? Can I save them? Maybe it's a premonition!

With the thought that she can put an end to these nightmares, Katlynn flings the blanket back and gets dressed.

She quickly heads to the front door where she slips on her boots, her coat, and her white gloves. Grabbing her keys, she leaves her house, bent on going to the pond.

****

Katlynn parks her car and gets out. The moon is quite bright, but she's still glad she brought her flashlight.

As she makes her way down to the skating area, a gust of wind whips past her. Katlynn stops and pulls her hood up, shoving her brown hair into it, and out of her face.

Her nerves make her shiver as she carefully starts out onto the ice. She shines her flashlight down, but the glare makes it hard to see.

Katlynn decides to get on her knees and crawl, sweeping the beam of light slowly, looking for any sign that someone is trapped below in the icy waters.

When she doesn't see anything, she moves forward and looks again. Ten minutes pass, and Katlynn questions if she'll ever find anything. She sits back and takes a moment; tears of frustration sting her cheeks.

She sees a shadow move nearby, followed by the sound of ice cracking. Katlynn swings her flashlight to the right. She catches the glimpse of a person falling into the water.

Katlynn jumps to her feet, nearly slipping and falling, but manages to stay upright. She hears them thumping the ice, followed by a loud, muffled yell.

"I'm coming!" she screams into the wind, doubting if the trapped person can hear her.

Moving on pure adrenaline, Katlynn makes her way to where the person went under, but the ice there is smooth. There's not a single crack.

She shines the flashlight around, but there's no evidence of anything having happened.

I saw someone, I know I did! Katlynn stomps her foot in frustration. *Ugh!*

The ice beneath her splits and gives way, plunging Katlynn into the freezing water below.

The cold shocks her for a moment before fear and instinct take over. Katlynn kicks her feet, surging her back towards the surface, but she's a bit off course and hits the sheet of ice.

Katlynn panics and thumps on it with her white-gloved hands. She gives out a muffled yell, choking on the water. Her hood falls back and her dark hair tangles around her face. She tries again to break the ice above her, growing weaker and weaker; eventually succumbing to the inevitable.

In the morning, her body is found by a shocked group of children. Katlynn's dead eyes stare through the ice. Her brown hair is matted around her face, and one white hand presses up, trying to escape the watery grave.

Gone

Light rose from the fire
Escaping into the darkness beyond

Shadowy figures gathered 'round the people
Who in turn, huddled around the flames

The sound of harmonious flutes heard thru the trees
Drowned out their whispered words

The people crowded together
But the light offered little comfort

Spirits, ghosts and specters danced merrily in the blaze
Leaping higher. Getting closer

Music from the woods grew and swelled
The group was trapped. No escape in any direction

The fire roared, lifting into a tremendous curtain
Then fell to ash, smoldering

The people were gone
As was the music, the flames, the darkness

Out To Sea

How long was he going to stay in here? How long could he? His food supply was running dangerously low, and if he ever wanted to get to land, he would have to steer.

The Maritime Dream had been out to sea for over a month when the trouble started.

Alan had no idea what disease had plagued the vessel and its crew. He managed to escape it, but only because he had stayed holed up in his cabin. He didn't even know if there were still survivors.

He had heard soft moans and whimpers when he'd risked opening his door two days ago, but there had been no footfalls to indicate any crew walking around since.

Alan had booked passage on the merchant ship, but only as a passenger. He did not know how to run the vessel, but if he was to live, it looked as if he would have to chance it.

Rising from the confines of his bed, he went to the door. Alan unlocked it, opening it only a crack. He pressed his ear to the gap before he thought it safe to step out.

The stench that hit him was overwhelming. Nausea quickly rose. He fought to keep the bile down.

Alan tore a piece of cloth off of his shirt and pressed it against his nose. He leaned on the wall until he could walk without feeling faint.

Bodies lay in the corridor; some half out of the rooms. He did his best to keep his eyes straight-ahead while he carefully picked his way around the corpses.

The last time he had been down this hall was when he had smuggled food and drink to his room, and had barricaded himself inside.

Many had still been alive then, but he had felt they would not be for long. They were fighting a losing battle. The sick had laid in their cots gasping for air and clawing at their skin, saying it burnt them.

Alan hadn't wanted to fall victim. The disease had terrified him, so he'd hid. And now... it seemed he was the only one left.

When he finally made it to the upper deck, he shoved the door open and inhaled a deep breath. The sea air stung, but was refreshing.

He pushed the door closed behind him. Leaning against it, Alan shut his eyes tight, as if that could force the images of the dead away.

After a few moments, he moved away from the door and took in his surroundings.

Several dead men lay on the deck, but the sky looked clear enough. Alan didn't have a plan to deal with an impending storm, as he knew very little about sailing. Instead, he focused on tasks he could do.

Alan began rolling the bodies on the deck overboard. He didn't want to have to stare at them until he found land, as well as worry about any lingering contagion that might still affect him.

With that job done, he headed into the captain's room and looked for anything he could use to board up the door leading below.

He couldn't stand to think about the state those corpses were in, and hoped that blocking the door might block the thought of them.

Once Alan was satisfied that the door was sealed, he moved any food and drink he could find from the captain's quarters to the helm. He used two belts lashed together to hold himself to the wheel, vowing to never completely let go until he was saved.

Days passed with Alan eating little, and sleeping even less. The wind and waves kept the vessel moving, but there had been no sighting of any land.

Exhaustion and worry were starting to take their toll. During the night, Alan thought he heard someone shuffling around on the deck with him, but had not seen anyone.

He tried to convince himself it was the spray from the ocean causing the noise, but wasn't so sure.

That afternoon as Alan started to nod off, the doorknob to the lower decks began to rattle. His head shot up and he looked at it.

Nothing further happened, and he turned back around to watch the ocean in front of the bow. An hour or two passed before he heard it again.

No one is alive, right? They've all surely perished, he thought.

The sound of the knob being twisted, and hands clawing at the wood, forced him to turn and look at the door again. This time, he saw the doorknob slowly rotate, but the boards held tight.

His eyes were wide with fright, and he felt sweat gather on his brow.

Were there indeed survivors? Did I lock them down there?

Alan strained his ears, but the noises had stopped.

"Hello?" he yelled. He waited, but there was no reply. He faced forward again, and undid the belts holding him upright. Once free, he stumbled and swayed, but eventually made his way to the door.

"Hello?" he called again. He pressed his head against the wood and listened intently. There was no sound, save for the waves hitting the ship.

He knocked on the door and shouted again. Nothing.

With uncertainty stamped across his face, Alan returned to the helm, and bound himself to the wheel. He placed his hands upon it, and continued his mission.

If someone is alive, the best I can do is get us to land, he told himself.

****

Night fell and Alan dozed. The belts held him upright. But nightmares plagued his dreams.

He heard whispers all around him calling him a coward, but what was he to do? He was no physician. How was he to help the sick and dying?

The voices didn't care. They followed him as he ran from them in his dream.

He woke with a start; his heart hammering in his chest. He looked around in the dark but couldn't figure out what had awoken him.

As he drifted back off, he heard it again. Fingernails scraping on wood.

Alan glanced at the lower deck door and heard someone moan in pain. A moment passed and he could smell death in the air. Turning his head away, he pressed a hand over his mouth and nose to block out the stench, but it didn't help.

Someone thumped against the wood, and one of the boards clattered to the ground behind Alan. He whipped his head around again to stare at the door in the gloom. It shook as someone struck it again, causing another board to fall.

Alan gripped the wheel tightly, and looked out over the sea. "I'm trying to get us to safety!" he screamed.

His confession seemed to make no difference. Another thump and another board down.

The doorknob rattled, and Alan heard the squeak of hinges.

With wide eyes, he looked back. The door was open, but no one was there. He glanced left and right, but saw no one… until he turned back around.

Dozens of crew members stood at the bow facing him. Their faces bloody and covered in sores. Their clothes tattered and ruined. They closed in around Alan, glaring at him.

"I'm trying to save us!" he yelled again, panic in his voice.

The crew said nothing, but one produced a knife, and used it to cut the belts holding Alan to the wheel.

Alan shrieked and tried to back away, but his tired legs gave out, and he landed on the deck. He scuttled backwards, away from the crowd.

They moved in closer, and closer, as he shifted away. Eventually, he found himself in the doorway to the lower deck. As soon as he crossed the threshold, the door slammed shut, trapping him below with the dead.

Alan screamed in the dark and beat on the door. But no one came to save him. Hands reached out from behind, gripping him tightly, and pulled him further into the bowels of the ship.

****

Morning came, and it brought the sight of land with it. A few hours later, the Maritime Dream ran aground.

By midafternoon, a salvage and rescue operation was underway to see what could be done about the ship and its crew.

They found no survivors and only dead bodies below deck, save for one corpse that was still lashed to the wheel.

The Trail

Seth strolls into the breakroom at work to grab something to drink from the vending machine. His friend, Bryan, comes in after him.

"How was your day off?" Bryan greets him.

"Good." Seth pulls his drink out of the machine and opens the top. "I found a new place to jog."

"Oh yeah? Where?" Bryan asks, his interest piqued.

"Over by the industrial park. I've driven past it before, but yesterday, I decided to check it out."

Seth takes a sip of his drink then notices his friend's face. "What?" he questions him.

"What was wrong with Hyde Park?" Bryan prods.

Seth shrugs. "Nothing. But a change of scenery is nice. And this place was actually pretty scenic."

"At the Industrial Walking Trail? I've heard things, man. Maybe stick to Hyde Park. It's safer there."

"Safer?" Seth quirks an eyebrow at his friend.

"Yeah, safer. And we're going to be late."

Seth glances at the clock. He takes another sip of his drink before following Bryan back to the loading docks.

****

After a few hours of unloading boxes and stocking shelves, Seth and his co-workers go to punch out.

"Hey, Bryan," Seth calls to his friend as he catches up to him. "What did you mean earlier about Hyde Park being safer?"

"Safer than what?" one of the other workers chimes in.

"Safer than jogging by the industrial park," Seth answers.

"Yeah, you don't want to go there," the co-worker warns.

Seth scoffs. "What is it about that place?"

"Look," Bryan states, "it's just that people go missing there. I mean, they could be dead, but the police never find a body."

Seth sees the worried faces around him, but he's skeptical. The trail seemed clean and safe to him.

"I don't mean to be rude," he says, "but you're making it sound like a ghost story. How many people have actually gone missing there? It's surrounded by businesses, and you can't really get lost. There's a path."

"I don't know," Bryan tells him. "I guess at least ten in the past few years. You should be careful if you're going to keep going there. If the police have checked it out, there's got to be something going on."

"Exactly," one of the others agrees. "Stick to Hyde Park."

****

On Seth's next day off, he drives over to Hyde Park. As soon as he pulls in, he starts thinking about the Industrial Walking Trail. Everyone at work had something to say about it.

Their tales only further intrigued him. It all just sounded like local lore. He even told them that. "Every town has someplace they claim is haunted. Doesn't mean it is," he had commented.

Now here he is, sitting in his car, facing Hyde Park. But he has to admit, he'd rather be at the trail.

After a few moments of hesitation, Seth puts his car in reverse, and backs out. He turns the wheel, puts the car into drive, and heads over to the Industrial Walking Trail.

****

The day is bright, the air is crisp, and the leaves are only beginning to fall off the trees. Seth stops his car on the side of the road, near one of the entrances to the walking trail. There are several cars parked at the buildings nearby, most likely belonging to the employees inside.

Seth shakes his head at the superstitions he's heard. *Maybe they've just never been out here,* he considers. *Their loss.*

He cuts the engine and gets out, then locks up and pockets his keys. Stepping onto the sidewalk he does a few stretches to loosen his muscles. He looks down the path, jogging in place for a moment.

Seems I'll have it all to myself, he thinks with a grin, heading down the trail.

As he jogs, he compares Hyde Park to the walking trail. He likes that this path is made of compact dirt and pebbles instead of asphalt.

And while the park is open and manicured, it's flat. Seth prefers the varying terrain of the trail, which begins to wind behind the buildings. As it does, the sound of the cars on the nearby highway fades into the background, while the noise of birds chittering in the trees seems to swell.

Seth's feet pound on the gravel, his breath coming in deeper huffs as he rounds a bend. The path slopes down towards a marshy meadow. He sees a bridge and a gazebo up ahead. He continues on his jog up a gentle hill to a small wooded area, where he turns back.

After twenty minutes, he slows down to a brisk walk. Reeds of grass sway in the light breeze, and the late blooming flowers on the hillside bend in the wind.

Seth lets his feet carry him back to the entrance he parked at. He doesn't encounter anyone today, but he didn't really expect to.

As he steps onto the sidewalk, he hears a short, scuffling sound behind him, and a great swarm of birds take flight with a *swoosh*. Seth flinches and looks back. He doesn't see a reason for the birds taking off.

He stands there watching them for a moment before pulling his keys out, and hopping into his car. He glances back down the trail. It looks so serene, just like the first time he came. Seth makes a mental plan to come back again.

****

Over the next several weeks, Seth opts to go to Hyde Park only once, returning, instead, to the Industrial Walking Trail on his days off. He usually starts closer to the bridge, but today he begins by the wooded area.

The wind blows a cool breeze and Seth picks up his pace. He pushes himself a little harder today. He makes it to the gazebo, then over the bridge before he turns around and jogs back.

As he nears the small woods again, he slows down, his breathing heavier. It's chillier here with the trees blocking out some of the sun, but the crunch of leaves under his feet makes Seth smile. He's always liked fall.

He watches a chipmunk scamper across the path, kicking up a few pebbles as it goes.

Once his breathing evens out, Seth hears the leaves rustle and then notices another sound. It's a sound he's heard before, the sound of someone briskly walking, their shoes scuffing the gravel. It's faint, but there.

Seth turns to look back, but can't see anyone. Parts of the path are obscured by the foliage and dips in the terrain. The shuffling sound seems closer, and is accompanied by the soft rustle of clothes moving.

He shrugs to himself and continues towards the end of the path. He finds the idea of someone else using the trail a good thing. *It's nice to know that not everyone is scared off by a story*, he thinks.

A cold wind stirs, and the birds in the trees still. The sound of dragging steps seems to be right behind him. Seth glances back over his shoulder, but the path is clear.

He stops, standing there with a frown on his face. The quiet scuffling fades away on the wind. A few gravel stones hit his shoe and Seth involuntarily jumps. His nerves are on edge. He dismisses the eerie feeling he has, reminding himself that sound travels, and another person on the path is a good thing.

A few leaves blow across the pebbled surface of the trail, and the birds begin to chirp again.

Seth turns back towards the entrance, and the road beyond. As he gets to his car, though, Seth swears he hears the gentle swishing of clothes, and the sound of shoes lumbering away from him.

****

"Please tell me you're not still going to the trail by the industrial park," Bryan questions Seth as they clock in.

"I am," Seth admits, "and nothing has happened. Maybe I should get a shirt that says 'I Survived The Trail'," he jokes.

"Ha," Bryan returns.

"You could come with me some time," Seth suggests. "See how peaceful and 'safe' it is. Besides, I'm not the only one who uses the trail. I've heard someone else walking it."

"How many times have you been there?" Bryan asks, concerned.

Seth thinks for a moment. "Um, about 5 times now."

"You're either brave, or stupid," Bryan tells him.

****

Seth pulls up to the curb and shuts off the engine. He's had a long week, and decided to jog after work for once. Only a few cars are in the surrounding parking lots, but there's still plenty of daylight left to enjoy.

Hopping out of his car and onto the sidewalk, Seth begins his stretches. He listens to the birds twittering in the trees that line the road.

After several minutes of warming up his muscles, Seth goes into a light jog, his feet following the gentle bend of the trail.

The foliage becomes denser as he heads away from the buildings. Small animals move in the undergrowth looking for something to eat. Seth takes a deep breath of fresh air. He doesn't understand how anyone could be afraid of this place. He finds it to be a refuge from city living.

On his return trip past the marshy area, he slows down to a walk, the sunlight just beginning to dim as twilight approaches. Seth's shoes crunch over leaves and gravel. The sounds of nearby traffic barely reach his ears.

The wind picks up for a moment, blowing the grass stalks together. A few pebbles shift under Seth's feet, and a grasshopper hops out of the way.

It takes him a moment to register an additional noise in the background, one that's coming from somewhere behind him. He's heard this shambling gait before.

It's just the walker, he tells himself, choosing to ignore it.

However, the noise will not be ignored. Seth hears it grow louder. He tries to keep his step the same speed, refusing to be frightened by someone walking. However, nerves get the best of him, and he begins jogging again.

He strains to listen for the footfalls behind him, hearing nothing at first. Then the crunching of leaves and the scuffing of shoes reaches him. His eyebrows furrow.

How can they be catching up to me? I'm jogging and it still just sounds as if they're walking.

His step falters, and he stops, heart hammering in his chest. The sound fades away, and he lets out a huff of air. Seth cranes his neck trying to see around the sloping hills and scattered trees, but nothing catches his eye. It seems like he's alone, but he doesn't feel alone.

Seth shakes away his unease, and continues walking. He makes it one full step before stopping again. Further up the path is a woman. She's standing there, looking at him. She doesn't move, but neither does he.

"Hi," he calls uncertainly, raising a hand in greeting. "Nice day."

She raises her hand, mirroring his action, and shouts back to him. "Hi. Nice day!"

Ookay, Seth thinks. "I was just finishing up," he yells. "Trail's all yours."

She parrots him again. His words coming back in her hoarse, phlegmy voice.

Not wanting to spend a second longer with this odd woman, Seth heads towards her with the intention of going around and getting quickly to his car.

As soon as he begins walking, she does, too. The woman moves swiftly, her shoes dragging on the dirt and gravel, a small grin on her face that widens as they get closer. Her bent arms pump in time with her step.

They start to pass each other, and Seth can't help but give her wide berth. He turns his head to watch her go. Her dead, milky white eyes meet his. Her grin stretches back in a grimace, exposing rotten teeth. She raises a hand in greeting again.

"HI! NICE DAY!" she screams at Seth, her rank odor hitting him full force.

He turns to run now, but she clamps an impressively strong hand on his arm, jerking him towards the tall grasses, and marshy ground beyond. He yells and yanks himself away from her, but she doesn't relent. Her slimy fingers tighten as Seth nearly escapes her grip.

He digs in with his feet and leans heavily away from her, trying to use his body weight to break free. She lets go and Seth lands with a grunt. His hands break some of the fall, but the air still rushes out of him. He quickly begins scrabbling away from her, struggling to find purchase on the trail.

She shuffles next to him and bends down, peering into his face. Her matted hair falls forward.

"Trail's all yours," she rasps at him.

He tries to back away, but with a blur of speed, she grabs him by the ankle and yanks him off the path. His scream causes the birds to take flight.

****

When the police are called in to investigate the car left by the path, they comb the trail for any sign of Seth. The only things they ever find are a few fingernails embedded in the gravel, and a torn jacket; snagged between some shrubs.

 Cold Revenge

Georg spotted Ulrich from across his tobacco field. He quickly mounted up and followed the man. But Ulrich had seen him as well and had urged his horse to quicken its pace.

The coward isn't going to get away that easily, Georg thought to himself. When he reached the small wooded area that caused the dirt road to bend and wind, Georg decided to cut through, requiring him to dismount and go on foot.

Ulrich heard boots crunching through snow, and saw branches being shoved aside. He reined his horse and clenched his jaw. *Fine.* If Georg wanted a confrontation so bad, he'd give him one, Ulrich decided, sliding to the ground. He'd just finished tying his horse up when Georg emerged onto the pathway.

"I will have my say, Ulrich! You will not come past my land and deny me!" Georg yelled.

Ulrich scoffed, and turned his back on his former friend. He pretended to busy himself by checking the reins, and straightening his frock coat; all to bide his time.

Georg stood there, seething with rage, waiting for the other man to turn around. Fists clenched and unclenched, and when Ulrich finally faced his foe, Georg punched him.

Ulrich stumbled back, his hand going to his jaw. He hadn't expected Georg to actually do anything. He was normally so meek.

Georg tensed, waiting for the other man to retaliate. Instead, Ulrich smirked at him.

Georg saw red and lunged at Ulrich. The two men grappled with each other, shoving and punching closer to the tree line. Ulrich tripped over the underbrush, falling back into the snow. Georg didn't relent. He kicked at Ulrich, who moved back and out of the way.

Ulrich managed to get back on his feet and shoved Georg against a tree. Snow rained down on them. A fierce wind blew through the small forest, and a noise came from above.

Both men paused for a moment in confusion, but Ulrich recognized the sound first. He held Georg where he was, only letting go when the cracking grew in intensity.

A large, snow-laden bough snapped off and fell on Georg, hitting and pinning him to the ground. Ulrich had managed to step back in time, leaving him unscathed.

Georg groaned and shifted beneath the branch and its many smaller offshoots. He lay on his stomach trying to regain his wits.

"Use this time to calm down, Georg," Ulrich warned. "This feud of ours is petty."

"Petty to whom?" Georg spat. "How you can see making underhanded deals with the bank as 'petty' is beyond me. You're trying to strip me of my property!"

Ulrich shrugged. "It is simply a business arrangement."

"One that will leave me destitute," Georg muttered. He tried to push the large branch off of himself, but to not avail.

Ulrich watched the fallen man struggle, taking a small amount of glee in the situation.

Georg attempted to find purchase in the snow, trying to pull himself forward, but didn't seem to make any headway. After a few tense moments, Ulrich decided to at least be civil.

"Shall I lend you a hand?" he offered.

Georg stopped and glared up at his foe, blood dripping into his eye from a headwound he did not know he had. "Help? From you!?" Georg's voice dripped acid. "I'd rather die."

"And so you may," a rebuked Ulrich said. He turned on his heel and marched back to his horse. He brushed the debris from his riding pants, remnants of their fight, and mounted his steed.

"You deserve this fate, not I!" Georg yelled from his prison.

"Perhaps I'll return later to check on you," Ulrich shouted back. "I'll at least send word to your estate upon my arrival at home, so they may look for you."

Georg bit back the retort on his lips, intent on freeing himself instead.

Ulrich waited a moment. He heard nothing but grunts and scuffling noises from the trapped man in the woods.

Feeling that he'd done his duty and was the bigger person for at least offering help, Ulrich urged his horse away from the scene. *It's not my fault if Georg is too stubborn to accept my assistance*, Ulrich rationalized.

However, a small sliver of guilt did persist in the back of his mind. It distracted him as he rode homeward.

When a pile of snow fell from a few branches onto the path, Ulrich was only loosely holding the reins. His horse spooked, rearing up enough to unseat Ulrich, who landed heavily on the ground.

A sharp pain pierced his side, and he twisted his wrist attempting to unsuccessfully catch himself.

He laid their momentarily, trying to get his bearings while his horse continued on without a rider.

Ulrich pushed himself back onto his feet. He stood there, swaying unsteadily, feeling a bit disoriented. *Had I hit my head when I fell? I don't remember doing so, but perhaps.*

Ulrich took a few ragged breaths, the pain in his side intensifying. He looked down the lane at the distant shape of his horse, and decided that the best course of action would be to return to Georg's estate, and perhaps release Georg from his confinement in the process.

Holding a hand gingerly to his ribs, Ulrich began his trek back to his former friend.

His movements were sluggish and clumsy as he walked along the road. The cold wind seeped in through his clothes, and Ulrich began to feel tired. He shook his head in an effort to stay awake. He was not far from where he had left Georg.

Ulrich thought about how grateful Georg would be to see him again.

Perhaps grateful enough to reasonably talk about my business arrangement, he mused.

Ulrich would even see to it that Georg got some of the proceeds, as his land was rich and fertile. *It should fetch a nice sum when divided up.*

Ulrich paused for a moment to catch his breath and was hit by a moment of clarity. He and Georg used to be so close. Ulrich couldn't even remember what slight had driven them apart, or why he felt the need to retaliate in such a manner.

He softly chuckled to himself, caught in his own lie. Ulrich could remember why he agreed to buy up Georg's land in such a scheme. The money he was to receive would pay off his debts, and see to it that his land appreciated in value.

Ulrich couldn't see passing up such an opportunity.

He continued walking down the lane, and when he saw the scuff marks in the snow, he knew he had reached his destination.

He moved towards the wooden area, taking another moment to rest against a tree. Guilt reared up.

Is this the same tree I forced Georg against?

Ulrich straightened up, the pain in his side briefly flaring to life. He coughed, not realizing that he expelled blood as he did so. The world grew fuzzy again, and he trudged forward.

Ulrich saw the large bough where Georg had lain, but his old companion was not there now. Judging by the disturbance in the snow, it looked as if help had come for Georg.

I suppose that's a good thing.

Ulrich sat down heavily on the cold ground. He barely shivered, his body numbing up. With a weary sigh, he leaned back on the heavy branch that had trapped Georg and shut his eyes. He felt worn out.

Ulrich thought of the pain Georg had been in as he struggled under the bough. *Why had I taken pleasure in that? How have I become this person?* he wondered.

He took shallow breaths, and groggily opened his eyes. Had he heard the crunch of boots on snow? Ulrich wasn't sure, so he lifted his head and looked around. He thought he saw Georg moving towards him.

The vision wavered and Georg disappeared.

Ulrich felt panic as he realized how dire his situation was.

"I'm sorry!" he yelled into the wind. He slumped back down as another bout of coughing racked his body.

Ulrich thought he heard the crunch of boots again. This time imagining they softly tread in front of him.

Ulrich turned his head to see the mirage of Georg in front of him.

"I *am* sorry," Ulrich whispered, his strength waning. He hoped his apology would mean something.

He envisioned Georg stretching out a hand to him in forgiveness. Ulrich reached out his own hand, but after a moment he realized it was a futile effort. There was no one there to save him.

Letting his hand drop down, Ulrich fell back against the branch and closed his eyes; one last time.

Uninvited

There's a… thing on my bed. It started showing up about a week ago.

It's not mine. I don't have any pets. And it's not a cat, though, I guess, it sort of resembles one, except…

Its head is bigger. And it sits like it's hunched over something, but I don't dare get close enough to see what.

It grins down at… whatever it sees on the comforter. Its eyes are always looking down. I don't see anything, but again, I don't get close enough, at least not while it's there. I never see anything on the blanket when it goes. What does it stare at?

It seems to have more hand than paw at the end of its front legs, and its tail is hypnotic in its slow back and forth swishing. I find myself just watching it…

Where was I? Oh, yes. Its tail. The sound of it sliding across the blanket makes my skin crawl. It almost sounds like scales catching on the fabric of my blanket.

I don't know why the thing is there. I see it before I leave for work; there, on my bed. I close the bedroom door and finish getting ready. It never follows. And it's still there when I return from work.

It's unnerving how it just stays there. But thankfully, it's always gone when I go to bed.

Should I try to lure it away? What if it comes back? I don't even know how it got in. I don't keep any windows open, and there aren't any large holes in the wall. I think I would've seen it if it had slipped in with me. That might have happened. But I don't think it did.

I've thought of asking someone else to come over, to see if they see it, too. But... But what if they don't? What then?

Forgive me. That yawn escaped. It's late and I'm tired. I should get some sleep. It should be gone, it's always gone by now. Though where it goes... I shudder to think.

I've looked under the couch, and I've searched the closets, and cabinets of my house. Not too well, mind you. I don't really want to come face to face with it.

It's not under the bed. That much I know. My mattress sits on a box spring, on the floor. Nothing could get under there. Right?

****

Wrong! Oh, so wrong! I was wrong. It... it can fit under the bed! I've watched it.

Yesterday I went to bed early for once. It was just getting up. I've never seen it move before. How do I explain it? It... unfolded itself.

It's taller than I thought, but still on all fours like a cat. And yes. Those are hands, not paws.

It walked like a cat. Right to the edge of the mattress, and then it jumped down. Its tail is long. The end of it was still on the blanket.

It stayed looking down. Its head never swaying or moving as it turned back towards the bed. Its tail eventually falling to the floor with a heavy **thump**. I flinched, but didn't move from my spot in the doorway. I just… I couldn't look away. I tried. Oh, I swear I tried.

It flattened like a shadow and then crawled under my bed. How do I sleep there now? How do I sleep at all?

I… I'm staying on the couch tonight. I slept there last night, too. What else can I do? I hate knowing that it was always in my room, even when I thought it wasn't.

****

I think I've angered it. I should've just slept in my bed. It's never bothered me there before, but now… *It's here.*

I don't want to open my eyes. I can hear its tail dragging on the carpet as it moves across the room. The sound is sickening.

Ah! It jumped onto my legs! It's heavier than I thought. What is it doing? What does it want? Why is it climbing closer? Please don't settle on my chest!

My breath hitches and it feels like it's getting heavier. I don't want to, but I'm going to risk cracking my eyes open. My eyelids widen on their own! I involuntarily jerk, trying to slide off the couch, but it grabs onto me, and suddenly I understand.

I know what it wants. *It wants me!*

Its eyes… Those eyes which are always looking down, are now… I'm under it! So now… now those eyes are looking directly at me!

And it's grinning. Is it happy? No. It's *Hungry!*

Shiver

She stood in the dark. Alone.

No one was here. She came by herself.

So who made that noise?

She spun to look, but saw nothing.

And who was that laughing?

The sounds quickly vanished.

A tap on her shoulder made her spin again.

A growl at her side. A chuckle behind her.

She turned and looked; saw nothing.

A scratch down her arm. A tingle up her spine.

Who's there? Where are you?

A puff of air on her neck ruffled her hair.

She looked everywhere she could. No one was there.

She was alone. She could see that much.

Then what was there in the dark?

She heard a breath. It moved in front of her.

She closed her eyes, covered her ears; and then...

She was gone.

The house empty again.

A giggle fading away.

Please like and review this book whereever you can, it really helps authors find more readers. Thank you ^_^

About The Author

Nicki Snyder currently lives in Wisconsin, which is where she settled after her mom retired from the Navy. And while she dislikes the cold, the beauty of the place, and the warmth of the people that she's met, keep her rooted there.

No Hope Beyond This Point is Nicki's fourth book. Her future writing plans include: additional children's books, a volume 2 to this book, and perhaps, someday, a novel.

In the meantime, she keeps busy with work, family, a menagerie of pets, and trying her hand at different ways to be creative.

You can check out her artwork online under **cannibalbananas** on most social media.

Other books published by Nicki Snyder:

The Circus Elephant

Howie

***Juanito y el Arbol* (Juanito and the Tree)**

At the time of publication: All books are available on Amazon and thru canbanarts.com